THE DEAD LETTER BOX

The idea came to Louie while she was lying in bed thinking about an old film that she had seen on the telly at Gran's. It showed how spies didn't send their letters through the post but left them in secret places, to be picked up later by their friends.

A dead letter box was just what Louie needed to keep in touch with *her* friend, Glenda, who had moved away to a new house. And she knew the perfect place for it: an old book in the library.

The story of how Louie leaves her secret letters in the library, with unexpected results, makes for an unusual, funny book that will be enjoyed by children up to nine.

Jan Mark comes from a London family, although she was born in Welwyn Garden City. She was educated at Ashford Grammar School and Canterbury College of Art. She began writing at an early age, winning second prize in a *Daily Mirror* short story competition at fifteen.

She now lives with her husband and two children in the Norfolk village of Ingham. Since their home is on the flight path of an RAF air base, she has become accustomed to aircraft spotting and this subject formed the background to her first book, *Thunder and Lightnings*, which won the Penguin/*Guardian* Award and the Carnegie Medal, and was runner-up for the *Guardian* Award for Children's Fiction.

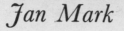

Jan Mark

THE
DEAD LETTER
BOX

Illustrated by Mary Rayner

PUFFIN BOOKS

PUFFIN BOOKS

Published by the Penguin Group
27 Wrights Lane, London w8 5tz, England
Viking Penguin Inc., 40 West 23rd Street, New York, New York 10010, USA
Penguin Books Australia Ltd, Ringwood, Victoria, Australia
Penguin Books Canada Ltd, 2801 John Street, Markham, Ontario, Canada l3r 1b4
Penguin Books (NZ) Ltd, 182 190 Wairau Road, Auckland 10, New Zealand

Penguin Books Ltd, Registered Offices: Harmondsworth, Middlesex, England

First published by Hamish Hamilton Children's Books 1982
Published in Puffin Books 1983
Reprinted in 1984, 1985, 1986, 1987, 1988

Made and printed in Great Britain by
Richard Clay Ltd, Bungay, Suffolk
Filmset in Monophoto Baskerville

Contents

Louie and Glenda

For five months now there had been a FOR SALE sign outside Glenda's house. Louie hardly noticed it any more; it had become part of the garden, like the concrete goblins, the bird-bath, and the green lamp post which grew up through the hedge; a tall tin plant with an orange flower on top that bloomed only at night.

Louie had forgotten that there was ever a time when the sign had not stood there, and she had begun to forget what it meant, so she was surprised one morning when she stopped on her way to school to wait for Glenda, and saw that the sign had changed. It no longer said FOR SALE. It said SOLD.

'You've sold your house,' Louie said, when Glenda came out through the gateway.

'Last week,' said Glenda. 'They only changed the sign yesterday.'

'You never told me.'

'I forgot.'

Louie remembered then what it was that *she* had forgotten: when Glenda's house was sold, Glenda would move away and Louie might never see her again, even though Glenda had been living at her end of the street as long as Louie had lived at the other. She had worked hard to forget it.

'If it was *me* I wouldn't have forgotten to tell *you*,' Louie complained, as they walked round the corner into Manor Drive.

'But you're not moving,' Glenda said.

'I might move one day. If I moved I'd tell you right away.'

'But I wouldn't be here,' said Glenda.

They were getting near the school, and people were turning into Manor Drive from all the other side roads. Glenda and Louie were best friends, but Glenda was Louie's only friend, while everybody was Glenda's friend. Glenda might start talking to almost anyone, even if Louie were already talking to her.

'When are you going?' Louie asked, quickly, but she was only just in time.

'In the holidays, I expect. Not till the end of term, anyway,' said Glenda, and hung back to talk to a girl from the top class who was coming up alongside them. Louie found that she was walking on her own, and started to hurry, so that people would think that she had left Glenda behind, and not that Glenda had left her in front.

Louie stood next to Glenda in Assembly, but there was no chance to talk

because they were in the choir and everyone could see them, up at the front. There was no chance to ask questions in class, because Glenda was on the other side of the room. Once they had sat at the same table, but Miss Ward said they talked too much, so now Louie had to share with Wayne Hodges, who wore his snorkel jacket indoors and sat with the hood zipped up, so that he looked like a ship's ventilator. Glenda was over by the window with Sarah and Helen Tate who were twins and talked only to each other, and Joanne Smith who sucked her pigtails and never talked at all.

Louie sat staring at the two shifty eyes that were Wayne, deep, deep inside his ventilator, and wondered what it would be like next term in Mrs Thomas's class, without Glenda. She would have to make another friend. She looked round the room to see who might do, but everybody had friends already. You could not go round saying to people, 'Will you be my friend?' They would giggle and say 'Why?' She

looked at Wayne again. Being friends with
Wayne would be like having a pet tortoise,
and she had a pet tortoise. Half the time it
wouldn't come out.

Miss Ward moved between the tables,
looking at people's work.

'Now, Michael, that's not very clever,
is it? Stop writing on your leg, Sarah.
Wayne, take your coat off – how many
more times? Yes, Glenda?'

'I've finished my card, Miss. Can I go
down the lib'ry, Miss?'

'Library, not liberry,' said Miss Ward.
'Say it properly.'

'Can I go down the *library*?' Glenda said, already half out of her seat. She always finished first, and she always ended the morning in the library, looking for a book to read, although she never seemed to find one. Louie watched her leave the room. In fifteen minutes the bell would ring. Glenda would rush home for lunch and not come back until it was time for afternoon lessons. Louie ate at school because her Mum was at work. At this rate she would never manage to speak to Glenda before home time, and then Glenda would be staying late for gymnastics, after school.

Louie had an idea, and hurried to finish her own work card.

'Can I go down the lib'ry, please, Miss?'

'Down *where*?'

'The lib'ry.'

'*Library*,' said Miss Ward. 'How many more times? Library, not liberry. It's not a fruit. It doesn't grow on a liberry bush. Li-bra-ree.'

'Can I?'

'All right. Off you go.' Louie went. Miss Ward was still at it as she left. 'Wayne, take your coat off. How many more times?'

'Here we go round the liberry bush, the liberry bush, the liberry bush,' sang Louie, under her breath, as she went down the corridor.

Glenda, looking very learned, was sitting on the carpet in the library area, with books piled all round her. She was reading a comic. Louie took a book from the nearest shelf and sat down beside her.

'You got finished quickly,' Glenda said, surprised. Louie usually finished everything last, because she sat and thought

about things instead of writing.

'I wanted to talk to you,' Louie said. 'When are you moving? Have you got a new house, yet?'

'I told you. In the holidays. We're going to live at Tokesby.'

'Near the sea?'

'That's right. My auntie lives there. We're going to have a bungalow. It won't cost as much as the house, so there'll be some money left over.' Glenda always seemed to know how much things cost. If she didn't, she asked. 'I might be able to have a pony.'

Glenda had wanted a pony for years. Louie also wanted a pony. She had once asked Mum about it.

'Where would we keep it?' said Mum. 'Under the stairs?' Louie didn't ask again.

'Can I come and see your pony?' she said. 'Sometimes?'

'I expect so,' said Glenda.

'I'll come and see *you*, anyway,' Louie said.

'I'll ask Mummy.'

'I'll ask my Mum if you can come and stay,' Louie said.

'My Mummy won't let me stay with people,' Glenda said. 'Not since I got the mumps off Julie Hodges after her party.'

'We can write to each other.'

'You write first,' said Glenda.

'I'll write the same day you move,' said Louie.

'Yes, well ... I haven't gone yet,' Glenda said.

2

I Spy

The library was Louie's favourite room at school, although it was not really a room at all, more like a large bite out of the side of the corridor opposite Mrs Thomas's office. The librarian was a boy in the top class, and Louie had decided to ask for the job when she too reached the top class, not next year, but the year after. She could see herself sitting at the wide wooden desk with the boxes of tickets on one side, the date stamp and ink pad on the other. Once, when the library was busy and no one was looking, she had stamped 7 MAY 1981 all the way up her arm, and Miss Ward had sent her to wash, and she had missed the book programme on telly. She would never forget the seventh of May.

In the meanwhile she spent all her free time there, but she was afraid that soon

she would have read all the books that
looked interesting and would have to
begin on the ones that did not. There were
two whole shelves of books that told you
how to do things. If anybody caught her
with one of those they would want to know
why she was not busy doing all the things
that the book was about. Louie preferred
thinking to doing. She knew that she could
never make a model Spitfire and fly it

down the rec., but she could easily imagine one and fly it in her head.

On Saturdays she went into the city with Mum to do the shopping, and spent an hour at the County Library, where they had so many books that she could never get through them all, even if she stayed in the children's library after she had grown up.

Given the chance, she would have spent Saturday afternoon reading the books that she borrowed in the morning, but while she was in the library, Mum was doing Gran's shopping, because Gran had trouble with her back, and on Saturday afternoon they took the shopping over to Gran who lived on the other side of the city. Mum would not let her read at Gran's.

'It's rude,' Mum said. 'You can't go into other people's houses and sit there reading. It's bad enough having you reading all over the place at home.'

Louie thought that probably Gran wouldn't give two hoots about it. Once upon a time, Gran had worked as a cleaner at the old library, so she couldn't mind books all that much, but Mum said what had that got to do with it? Just because you were a cleaner in a fish shop, said Mum, it didn't mean that you had to eat fish all the time, so on Saturday afternoons Louie sat in the living room with Gran's budgie, and watched old films on television, while Gran and Mum went

through the shopping, item by item, and Gran complained about the prices.

It was six weeks now since the SOLD notice had gone up in Glenda's garden. The summer holidays had begun and every morning Louie ran to the gate and looked up the road to see if there was a removal van parked outside Glenda's house, but so far she had seen only Glenda's dad's car and her brother's old van that wouldn't start without jump leads and someone else's battery.

She hardly ever saw Glenda at all. Glenda was busy packing. But one Saturday afternoon, as Louie was walking back from the bus stop in Manor Drive, with Mum, after a visit to Gran's, Glenda leaned over the gate and said, 'I've been looking for you for ages. We're going next week.'

Louie stopped and put down her carrier bag of library books.

'What day?'

'Thursday.'

'I thought you must have gone already,' said Louie. 'I haven't seen you for days.' She hoped Glenda would notice how sarcastic she sounded.

'We've been over at the bungalow.' If Louie hadn't known that a bungalow is just a particularly squat kind of house, she would have guessed that it was something like Buckingham Palace, the way Glenda went on about it. 'And I went to look at the school,' said Glenda. 'It's ever so small. I'll be going there, next term.'

'I bet they close it, soon as you get there,' Louie said, nastily.

'Why?'

'They always close little village schools. Then there's letters in the paper, and people moaning about it on telly, but it's no good. They never open them again. I bet they close yours. I bet you have to go to another school miles and miles away – *by bus*!'

'There's a field next to the bungalow,' Glenda said, calmly. 'With a shed in it. Just big enough for a stable.'

'Are you staying there all night?' Louie's mother yelled. She was half way down the road, and had only just noticed that Louie was no longer behind her.

'Will you be coming into the city for

shopping, when you move?' Louie said, in a hurry. 'We could meet each other, sometimes.'

'On Saturdays, Mummy said.'

'Well, so do I. We could meet at the library, on Saturday mornings.'

'We'll be coming on Saturday after-noons,' said Glenda.

'Louie! *Will* you get a move on?' Mum was shouting, right down by the pillar box now.

'I've got to go,' Louie said, panicking.

'Bye-bye,' said Glenda.

Louie realized that unless she did something about it, things would be exactly the same next Thursday. Glenda would say 'Bye-bye,' climb into the car and disappear for ever.

'I'll come down yours in the morning,' she said, gathering up the books.

'I'll be busy in the morning,' said Glenda. 'Packing and that.'

'Just for ten minutes – I've *got* to see you,' Louie said. 'I've had this terrific idea.' She left Glenda at the gate and ran after Mum. It was not true about the terrific idea; she had not had one, but she would have done by the time she saw Glenda on Sunday morning. She was sure of that. She always had more ideas than she knew what to do with.

The idea came to her in bed, while she was thinking about the old film that she had seen on the telly at Gran's. It had been about spies, and was so complicated that for most of the time she'd had not the faintest idea of what was going on, especially after switching on late and finding a

dead man already falling downstairs, head over heels. One spy had spent a great deal of time writing letters full of Government secrets and sending them to the enemy. Louie had been thinking a lot about letters recently. Glenda had agreed that they should write to each other, but Louie had a feeling that *she* would be doing most of the writing, and stamps were expensive. Glenda might have plenty of money, but she probably would not want to spend it on letters to Louie. Louie simply did not have much money. The only way to make sure that Glenda wrote to her was to make a game of it, and this was where the spy came in.

The spy had not put stamps on his letters and posted them into a pillar box. He had hidden them in a hollow tree on Hampstead Heath, which seemed to be in London although it looked like the middle of the country. Later on, the enemy had come by, quite ordinary and respectable, with a spaniel on a lead, and had taken the letters out again. The man who finally

caught the spy called the hollow tree a
dead letter box. Louie could not see what
was dead about it because although
hollow, it still had plenty of leaves, but it
was a good idea, all the same. She and
Glenda would have a dead letter box, and
she knew exactly where it would be.

3

Going, going . . .

Glenda's house was full of tea chests on Sunday morning, and Glenda's mother made Louie and Glenda go and talk in the back garden while she ran about filling the tea chests with clothes and crockery, in padded sandwiches, making lists, and then taking everything out again and putting it somewhere else.

'You'd better be quick,' said Glenda. 'I ought to be helping.'

'I had this idea,' said Louie. 'I saw this film yesterday, on telly.'

'So did I,' Glenda said. 'Mummy says I can choose my own curtains in the new bungalow. And a lampshade to match. It won't half be funny, sleeping downstairs.'

'Not if you haven't got an upstairs,' Louie pointed out. 'I meant the film about the spies. Is that the one you saw?'

'Yes, only it was dead boring, so I

switched over to the racing.'

'*Motor* racing?'

'No, horses, of course.'

'Did you see that bit about leaving letters in a hollow tree on Hampstead
Heath?'

'No, look' – Glenda sounded just like her mother, – 'I can't stand around here all day, talking about old films.' Louie moved quickly so that she stood between Glenda and the back door.

'There was this spy, see, and he knew people were opening his letters and that, so he stopped posting them and hid them in this tree, and then this other spy took his dog for a walk and got the letters out again, and nobody knew. I thought we could do that.'

'We haven't got a dog,' said Glenda. 'Anyway, I'm moving on Thursday.'

'I know you are. But you said you'd be

coming into town on Saturdays, for shopping.'

'I shan't see you,' Glenda said, firmly. 'We're coming in the afternoons.'

'*I know.* You said. But we could have a dead letter box, too, like they did in the film. I could leave a message for you in the morning, and you could collect it in the afternoon and leave one for me.'

Glenda began to look faintly interested. 'Where'd you leave it?'

'In the library,' Louie said.

'I don't belong to the library,' said Glenda.

'You could join.'

'I don't want to join.'

'Well, you needn't, not if it's only to collect letters. You can just go in. Anyone can go in. It's free.'

'It's on the rates,' said Glenda, knowingly. 'Mummy said. Look, where would you leave this letter, then?'

'I don't know. In a secret place,' Louie said, wondering where she would find a secret place in the County Library, always full of people.

'But you only go to the library on Saturdays,' said Glenda. 'I'll be gone by next Saturday. I won't know where you've left it.'

'I'll go in tomorrow, then,' Louie said, recklessly, not at all sure that Mum would let her go into the city alone, 'and I'll find a dead letter box and tell you about it before you go. Then you'll know where to look. All right?'

'All right,' Glenda said. 'But I might forget.'

The County Library stood between the Theatre Royal and City Hall, opposite the car park. At the bottom of the steps that led up to the entrance was a little shrubby tree growing inside a collar of brown cobble stones. This, thought Louie, could be the liberry bush. In spring there were clusters of pink flowers hanging from the branches but, unfortunately, no berries in winter; nothing you could make into liberry jam.

Louie had to go downstairs to reach the children's library, in the basement. The adult library was on ground level and where the stairs went down there was a kind of balcony and a railing along the side where you could lean over and watch the people down below in the children's section. When she had finished choosing her books, Louie liked to go back upstairs and lean over the railings, pretending that she was on the verandah of a house built onto a mountainside in wild foreign parts, or on the bridge of a star ship, gazing out over the universe, or in a skyscraper, in New York, or just enjoying the thought that, if she wanted to, she could spit on someone's head; but this morning there was no time for that. Mum had not been very pleased about her going to the city alone, and she had to be home by twelve o'clock. Also she had had to use most of that week's pocket money on the bus fare, as Mum would not let her walk so far by herself. She went straight down the stairs and began to look for somewhere to use as a dead letter box.

The children's library was disguised as a big living room, with pictures on the walls, and a carpet, and canvas bean bags, big enough to sit on, in case people got frightened by seeing so many books, and went away again without reading anything. No one could say you were rude if you sat reading in this living room, and it was not like a book shop where people grew suspicious if you stood around just looking, and didn't buy anything.

Louie stood around just looking. The first place she thought of was the card index, with all its little drawers, so long and narrow, that slid out silently when she pulled the handles. The cards, on their brass spindles, did not go all the way to the backs of the drawers. There was quite a big gap in some of them, where a letter would fit nicely and never be found except by someone who was looking for it. But as she watched, one of the librarians took out the A–L drawer and unscrewed the spindle. All she wanted to do was put some more cards in, but in so doing she found an old sweet wrapper that someone had hidden there, and crossly took it out. That might easily happen to a letter. Louie moved away.

She wondered if it would be possible to hide a letter behind one of the shelves, against the wall, but Glenda might forget where she was supposed to look, or get

tired of searching. Someone might mistake
it for rubbish and throw it away.

While she was examining the shelves

Louie noticed that one very thin book had slipped behind the others. She took it out and looked at the author's name, so that she could put it back in the right place. It was called *The Windmill Children*, by Penelope Saltash. Louie had never heard of Penelope Saltash, so she looked inside. It did not seem to be a very popular book. There were no fingerprints in it, or dog-eared pages, but when she leafed through it, an old bus ticket fell out. She picked it up and looked at it to see if the numbers added up to seven, which was lucky. They came to twenty-three, which was neither here nor there. She looked at the date: 7 May, the day that she had date-stamped her arm. Perhaps that was lucky too. Then she looked at the last date on the slip at the front of the book: 7 MAY 1977. All those sevens had to be lucky, but it was more than four years ago. No one had borrowed the book for four years. Perhaps no one would ever borrow it again. It was the perfect place to leave a

dead letter – in the little pocket at the front, where the ticket went.

Even if someone picked it up and looked at it, they would never find a letter hidden there. It was the perfect dead letter box. Better than that, it was a dead letter book.

4

Gone

On Thursday Glenda moved.

Louie hung over her front gate as the car went by, but Glenda was not looking in the right direction and she disappeared round the corner without seeing Louie at all. Louie walked up the road and looked at Glenda's empty house. Three giant sunflowers stared back at her over the high side gate, and the moon-flower lamp post looked down at her from where it stood in the privet hedge that no one had bothered to trim for weeks. The concrete goblins had gone in the removal van, and the bird bath was dry. There were weeds in the cracks of the crazy paving. The house looked as if it had been empty for ever, instead of half an hour.

Louie went home and wrote a letter to Glenda, ready to leave in the dead letter book on Saturday. It took her a long time

because she could not think of anything to say. She wrote 'Dear Glenda', and then sat at the kitchen table, gnawing the rubber at the end of her pencil, and wondering what she and Glenda used to talk about. She could not remember Glenda ever saying anything except yes and no and, more often, perhaps. In the end she wrote,

Have you got your pony yet? I hope you like your new bungalow. I hope I can

come and see you soon. DON'T FORGET
TO ANSWER THIS LETTER!!!
Love, Louie.

There was no chance that Glenda
would have her pony by Saturday, but it
would give her something to write back
about, even if she only said *No*.

On Saturday morning Louie and Mum
walked up to Manor Drive to catch the

bus into the city. The SOLD sign had gone from the garden that had been Glenda's, and there was a stack of buckets and ladders and paint cans by the front door. Whoever had bought the house didn't like the colour that Glenda's dad had painted it.

When they got off the bus Mum went

down to the market place, while Louie took her carrier bag of books and went off across the car park, past City Hall, three times round the liberry bush for good luck, and into the library.

When she had handed the books back to the librarian, behind the desk at the foot of the stairs, she went at once to the shelf where she had found the dead letter book. It was still there, just where she had left it, but a big hand-woven lady with four dribbly children was shoving up alongside, so until it was safe to put back *The Windmill Children* with the dead letter inside it, she went and checked in the card index, to see if Penelope Saltash had written any other books. She had not. There was only one card with her name on it. Perhaps she had got tired of writing books when no one bothered to read *The Windmill Children*. Poor Penelope Saltash.

When the lady and the children had moved on, Louie went back to the shelf, opened up *The Windmill Children* and tucked her letter, folded very small, into

the little pocket at the front. Then she put it back tidily on the shelf, between books by people called Saddler and Samuels, where Glenda would be sure to see it; so long as Glenda had kept the bit of paper that Louie had given her, with the name of the book on it. She would never remember, otherwise.

*

There was no television at Gran's that afternoon. The set had broken down, and no one could come to mend it until Monday. Louie sat on the settee and looked sideways into her carrier bag, where the books were waiting.

'Let her read if she wants to,' Gran said. 'I don't mind.'

'You can't get any sense out of her when she's got her head in a book,' Mum said. 'I keep telling her it's rude, but she doesn't take any notice.'

'It's no ruder than watching telly all the time,' Gran retorted. Louie pretended not to hear. It sounded almost as if Gran were telling Mum off. She shook all the books, one after the other, to see if there were any more bus tickets inside.

'What are you looking for?' Gran asked. 'Money?'

'Bus tickets,' Louie said. 'People put them in for bookmarks, and forget about them.'

'When I was a cleaner down the old library, after the war, they used to have a

whole shelf of things that people left in
books,' said Gran.

'Was there ever any money?' Louie
asked, and gave the second book another,
extra hard, shake, in case there was a
pound note inside.

'Once or twice, but it was usually

something much worse,' Gran said. 'They found a kipper bone in one, and a rasher of streaky bacon inside *Wolff's Anatomy for Artists*. I remember that particularly. It matched the pictures.'

'You wouldn't catch anyone doing that these days,' said Mum. 'Bacon's that dear it would be cheaper to leave money.'

'It would be cheaper to eat books,' said Gran.

Louie imagined a paperback lying like a slice of bread in the frying pan, between two tomato halves and an egg. The fat began to bubble. The book sizzled. Its pages opened and closed a few times, then turned brown and curled up crisply along the edges. Fried book: she could almost taste it.

A bus ticket fluttered out of the last book, onto her lap, and the numbers added up to fourteen – twice seven. That might be twice as lucky. Louie hoped it meant that Glenda was at that very moment searching for her letter.

*

Louie would have liked to go back to the library on Monday to see what Glenda had left in the dead letter book, but Mum would not let her walk, and she had no money left for the bus fare, so she had to wait.

The time passed very slowly. Every day she went up the road to see what was happening to Glenda's house. The new owners were very busy, painting the doors and

window frames bright red. They painted the bricks red, too, and drew white lines between them, along the mortar. Inside, green curtains went up at the windows. Louie thought of Glenda choosing her new curtains, and a lampshade to match. On Thursday the bird bath was taken away in a barrow, and on Friday there was another removal van parked at the kerb. Louie hung about all morning and watched the furniture go in; gas stove, kitchen stools, a refrigerator, a three piece suite, chairs, tables and a wardrobe, but all of it large and heavy, and there was only one bed.

Louie could guess that there would be no children, but by now she had read her three books, one of them twice, and it was nearly time to go back to the library.

5

Death of a Letter

'Here we go round the liberry bush,' sang Louie, on Saturday morning, and went round the liberry bush, three times for luck, swinging her books in the carrier bag.

The librarian on duty knew Louie by name, probably because Louie showed up at exactly the same time every week. Louie handed over the books, parting reluctantly with the one she had read twice because she was longing to read it again, but could not bear to pass up the chance of a new one, took her tickets and went straight over to the 'S' shelf. *The Windmill Children* was still there, between Saddler and Samuels. Louie looked round to make sure that no one was watching and, opening the book, poked her finger into the little pocket at the front. There was something in it, tucked down at the bottom below the slip of card with the book's name typed on it. Glenda had not forgotten, then. Louie drew out the folded paper between two fingers, and opened it.

It was her own letter.

At first she thought that Glenda must have left it there by accident, and she pushed her fingers back into the pocket, searching for another piece of paper, but there was nothing else there. She thought then that she was going to cry. Not only had Glenda not bothered to answer Louie's letter, she had not even bothered to look for it. Glenda had gone off to the new bungalow and the field with a shed in it that was just big enough for a stable, and forgotten all about her.

Louie sat down on one of the bean bags, took a pencil out of her pocket, and began to write a second letter on the back of the first one.

It was much easier to write than the first letter.

She folded it up again and put it back in the little pocket and closed the book. The library was almost empty now except for a thin girl in glasses, playing with the card index. Louie stood up, put *The Windmill Children* on the 'S' shelf, care-

Dear Glenda,

I think you are a
Mean Rotten Old Thingy and
I never did like you. I'm
GLAD you moved. I wish
you moved years ago. They
have painted your house
HORRIBLE RED all
over and thrown the
bird bath away. I hope
you DONT EVER
come back.

Love from Louie.

lessly, between Stevenson and Stewart, and pretended to be looking for more books, but all the colours on the spines turned wet and misty, and began to run, like the time Wayne Hodges, blinkered in his snorkel, had upset his paint water all over her picture at school. It had been a painting of a library with rows and rows of lovely books, all different colours like striped liquorice allsorts – until Wayne overturned his jam jar.

She walked all round the shelves, blinking and sniffing, while the books dried out. On one wall was a big sheet of peg board, with wire brackets stuck into it, where the librarians put new books that they thought people might like to know about. Louie paused to glance at it, stopped and stared, and stared again. There on a bracket, right in the middle of the peg board, was *The Windmill Children*, by Penelope Saltash.

She took it down and looked inside, to see if it really was the same one. There was no doubt about it; her letter was in the little pocket at the front. The librarian must have decided that it was time somebody read *The Windmill Children*. Louie looked round guiltily, but the librarian was busy at the desk where a queue had suddenly formed. She put the book back on the 'S' shelf, and was about to walk away when a voice said, 'What did you go and do that for?'

Louie turned in a fright, thinking that another librarian must have been watching her, like the hero watching the spy in the film, but the only person who could have spoken was the girl in glasses who had been looking at the card index.

'Why did you take that book down off the peg board?' the girl asked, and pulled it from the shelf.

'I thought it was there by mistake,' Louie muttered. 'That board's for new books. Nobody ever reads this old thing.'

'I know,' the girl said. 'That's why I put it there.'

'You put it there?' The girl could only be a year or two older than Louie. Perhaps she was a sort of dwarf librarian, starting young and working her way up.

'Yes. Why not? I often put books up there if they never get borrowed. *The Windmill Children*'s got an awful cover and no pictures, so no one wants it, but if it's up on the board someone might think it's good and take it home.'

'You're not supposed to do that, are you?' Louie asked. 'Don't they stop you?'

'They don't see me,' said the girl. 'I do it all the time with my mother's books, just to make sure they get noticed. Put it back.'

She pushed the book into Louie's hand. Louie stood and stared at it.

'Does your Mum write books? Did she write this one?'

'No – she's better than that,' said the girl. 'But this isn't too bad. Go on, put it back.'

'I can't,' Louie said. 'It's my dead letter box.'

'Your what?'

'Like spies have,' Louie said. 'I put a

letter in here, and my friend collects it
and leaves one for me. At least, she was
supposed to,' said Louie, 'but she forgot.
Or didn't bother.'

'I never thought of that,' the girl said.
She took the book from Louie and opened
it. 'Where's the letter?'

'In that little pocket at the front. Are

any of your Mum's books down here? What's her name?'

'No, they're all upstairs in the adult section,' the girl said. 'She's Mary Garland.'

Louie wished that she had heard of Mary Garland. 'What's your name?'

'Jane Garland.' Jane was reading the letters. 'Are you sure this Glenda's your friend?'

'She used to be,' Louie said, 'till last week, but she's got a bungalow now.'

'I'd tell her to go and chase herself,' said Jane. 'I'd tell her to take a long walk off a short pier. If people don't answer my letters I ring them up and bawl them out.'

'I haven't got a phone,' said Louie. 'And *she's* having one, but I don't know the number. She didn't even tell me her address.' She looked at the book and the colours began to run again.

'Well, let her get on with it. You've got other friends, haven't you?'

'No,' Louie said. 'Well, Wayne Hodges

is all right, but he won't unzip his snorkel.
You can't talk to him. He never hears
what you say, half the time.'

'You want to advertise,' Jane said.
'How?'

'Like those postcards in little glass cages
outside shops. If people want something
they write an advert on a postcard, and
the shopkeeper puts it up for them. We
did that when we lost our cat, and
someone brought him back.'

'It would cost too much,' Louie said.

'I didn't mean *you* should write a post-card. Put a message in a book, only don't hide it this time. If you leave an address, someone may find it and write to you. It would be like getting a pen friend.'

'Suppose it was someone I didn't like?'

Jane thought about that. 'Put it in a book you enjoy, and the right sort of

person will find it. Look, I'll help you. Have you got any more paper?'

They sat down on the same bean bag and planned an advertisement.

My name is Louise Cossey. I live at 68, Cromer Road. Please write to me if you would like to be my pen friend. I think this is a good book, don't you?

'What if nobody answers?' said Louie.

'Bring some more paper next week and write lots of them,' Jane said. 'Someone's sure to answer in the end.'

They put the note into one of Louie's favourite books and stood it on a bracket in place of *The Windmill Children*, which went back between Saddler and Samuels.

'Have you ever read *The Windmill Children*?' Jane asked.

'No.'

'Well, why don't you?'

'Next week,' said Louie. 'I'll leave it for now. Glenda might come in after all, this afternoon, and I'd like her to see what I wrote.'

6

Liberry Jam

It was only after Jane had left that Louie realized that she did not know where Jane lived. She ran up the stairs, after her, but Jane was already tacking through the crowds in the adult library. She slipped through the double doors and down the steps, past the liberry bush. Louie lost sight of her after that, among the cars in the car park.

Then, for the first time, she ventured among the shelves in the adult library, and looked in the history section for Mary Garland's books. She did not have far to look. They were all on display on brackets, or standing up on top of shelves, where people would notice them. Jane had been at work.

Louie waited all week to see if anyone would write, waylaying the postman at the gate, but there were never any letters

for her. Glenda was choosing curtains and lampshades away in the bungalow and no one, it seemed, had answered her advertisement.

'I'll be glad when you go back to school,' Mum said on Saturday morning. 'You're like a flea in a fit, these days. Stop fiddling with those letters and put your shoes on. You're not going to town in your socks.'

The first person she saw in the library was Jane, lurking about near the head of the stairs, where the history books were kept.

'Did you get any letters?' Jane asked at once, before Louie had had time to say hello.

'Not yet,' Louie said. They went downstairs and looked for *The Windmill Children*. It was still there, and Louie's letter to Glenda was still inside, undisturbed since last week. Louie said nothing, but while the librarian was looking the other way she took out the letter and put *The Windmill Children* on a bracket against the peg board.

'I bet someone borrows it now,' said

Jane. 'We put your advertisement book there and that went on Monday.'

'How do you know it was Monday?'

'I came in to check. I come every day, nearly. I'm going to try advertising too,' Jane said, and took a bundle of notes out of her pocket. Every time she opened a book to look inside she slipped a note into the last chapter.

Louie squinted over her shoulder, and read;

If you enjoyed this book, please write to Jane Garland, 105, Corunna Gardens, London, W9. I enjoyed it too.

'London? You've come all the way from London?'

'I'm on holiday,' Jane said, 'staying with my cousins.'

'Oh.' Louie felt disappointed, without having realized that there was anything to be disappointed about. 'When are you going home?'

'In September.'

'When will you come back again?'

'I don't know. After Christmas, per-haps. Maybe at Easter. I'm only here now because Mum's away lecturing in America. Come on, aren't you going to put any ads in?'

Louie opened a few books and slipped her advertisements inside, without even bothering to look at the titles. First

Glenda, then Jane: everybody went away and Louie was always left behind. One day, she wouldn't be surprised, she would peer into the depths of Wayne's snorkel and find that he had gone too, in the middle of arithmetic, while no one was looking.

When Louie met Mum at the steps by the market, Jane went off to the bookshop in St Giles Lane, to make sure that all her mother's books were at the front of the shelves.

'Who was that you were with?' Mum said.

'Jane Garland. I see her in the library sometimes. Her mum writes books,' said Louie.

'That's what she tells you,' said Mum.

'I've seen the books,' said Louie.

'Trust you to find someone whose mother writes books,' Mum said. 'Did you tell her your mother works in Tesco's?'

'She didn't ask,' Louie said. 'But I told

her about Gran being a cleaner at the old library.'

'And what did she say to that?'

'She didn't say anything. I told her about the bacon bookmark, and she said her Mum once found half a poppodum in an Agatha Christie. What's a poppodum?'

'Some people always have to go one better. It's an Indian pancake,' said Mum. 'Sort of. Anyway, you won't be going to the library next week. One of your dad's mates is lending us his caravan at Clacton, for the weekend.'

The caravan was supposed to be a rare treat. Louie had to look pleased.

She was sure it would rain all the time they were at Clacton, but it was hot and sunny, and she spent the whole weekend on the beach with her three library books that she had been saving specially. She hoped there would be a pile of letters on the doormat when she came home, in answer to her advertisement, but there was only one postcard, from Auntie Pauline, on holiday in Majorca.

'Some people,' said Mum, 'always have to go one better.'

There was nothing from Glenda; nothing at all for Louie.

They came home on Sunday night, and there were still five days to go before she could get to the library again. Next morning she went up the road to see how the house was coming along. The sunflowers were still drooping over the side gate, but the house, red and glistening all over, looked like a model of a house; the kind you press out and fit together without glue, that always fall to bits very quickly. A lady she had never seen before was trimming the privet hedge round the lamp post.

Louie said 'Hello.' The lady said 'Good morning,' and went on cutting the privet.

On Saturday she ran all the way from the bus stop to the library and found Jane outside going round and round the liberry bush.

'Where were you last week?' Jane said.

'I had to go on holiday,' said Louie. 'It was a surprise. I didn't want to.'

'I was afraid I wouldn't see you again. I'm going home tomorrow,' said Jane.

'Already?'

'School starts next week.'

September already. Things were going from bad to worse. 'Have you had any letters yet?' Louie said. She could not think of anything else to say.

'I might have, I don't know. They'll all

be in London if I have, won't they? Waiting for me,' she said, happily. 'What about you?'

'No. Nothing. Not yet.'

'Well, you never know your luck,' said Jane. 'The library's ever so full, today. There's a queue on the stairs.'

There was, too, as far as the bend, half way down. Jane and Louie had to tag on at the end of it and wait for five minutes before they could get to the desk. Louie handed over her books and they pushed their way in. She had never seen the library so full. There were children everywhere, standing at the shelves, squatting on the floor, and squeezed together, three to a bean bag, on the carpet, but nobody was reading. They were all opening books and taking out bits of paper. There were bits of paper all over the floor. People were swapping bits of paper and copying down addresses. Others were looking for empty books to put their addresses into. Two librarians were standing by the desk, looking both interested and worried.

'Cor,' said Jane. 'We did that.'

'Dead letter books,' said Louie.

'It's a whole cemetery,' Jane said. 'I think we ought to go before someone remembers us.' They wriggled out again and went quietly upstairs. Louie paused at the bend.

'All those people,' she said, sadly, 'and nobody wrote to me. It was my advert that started it.'

'Oh, well,' Jane said, 'you don't really need to advertise for a friend now, do you?

You've got me.'

Louie had not thought of that. 'But you live in London. You're going away.'

'We can write, can't we? I *always* answer letters,' said Jane. 'Once a month, eh? or we'll get bored and stop bothering.'

Louie nodded. She could afford a stamp once a month. They pushed their way clear at the head of the stairs and met a fresh surge of children on the way down. Through it the head librarian of all the library was wading toward them.

'Traffic jam,' Jane said, 'and here comes the traffic warden. Scarper.'

Louie turned back for a moment to look down into the children's library. She could not see the floor. The room was full of heads, seething like fruit in a saucepan, at a rolling boil.

'No,' she said, 'not traffic jam; liberry jam,' and they went out, down the steps, three times round the liberry bush for luck, and into the car park.

PROFESSOR BRANESTAWM'S POCKET MOTOR CAR
Norman Hunter

Two Branestawm stories specially written for younger readers: the Professor's amazing genius for invention produces an inflatable car to solve parking problems, and an extremely clever letter-writing machine.

CHANGING OF THE GUARD and WALLPAPER HOLIDAY
H. E. Todd

Two delightful stories about the adventures of Timothy Trumper and his family. Ideal for reading aloud.

MEET MARY KATE
MARY KATE AND THE SCHOOL BUS
MARY KATE AND THE JUMBLE BEAR
Helen Morgan

True to life stories of a happy four-year-old's busy days at home and her first steps into the interesting world of school.

KATY AND THE NURGLA
Harry Secombe

Katy had the whole beach to herself, until an old, tired
monster swam up to the very rocks where she was sitting
reading. Harry Secombe's first book for children has all the
best ingredients in the right proportions: a monster, a space-
ship, adventure, humour and more than a touch of happy
sadness.

THE WORST WITCH
THE WORST WITCH STRIKES
AGAIN
A BAD SPELL FOR THE WORST
WITCH
Jill Murphy

Mildred Hubble is the most disastrous dunce of all at Miss
Cackle's training school for witches. But even the worst witch
scores the occasional triumph!

MOULDY'S ORPHAN
Gillian Avery

Mouldy dreams of adopting a poor orphan, someone to keep
warm and happy ever after – but when she finally finds one
and brings him home to their crowded cottage, Mum and
Dad aren't pleased at all.

DAVID AND HIS GRANDFATHER
Pamela Rogers

Three stories about David and his kind grandfather, who participates in all his secret schemes.

IT'S TOO FRIGHTENING FOR ME!
Shirley Hughes

Down by the railway a white face looks out of a spooky old house, and Jim and Arthur hardly dare investigate.

TALES FROM ALLOTMENT LANE SCHOOL
Margaret Joy

Twelve delightful stories, bright, light and funny, about the children in Miss Mee's class at Allotment Lane School. Meet Ian, the avid collector; meet Mary and Gary, who have busy mornings taking messages; and meet the school caterpillars who disappear and turn up again in surprising circumstances.

WORD PARTY
Richard Edwards

A delightful collection of poems – lively, snappy and easy to read.

THE THREE AND MANY WISHES OF JASON REID
Hazel Hutchins

Jason is eleven and a very good thinker so when he is granted three wishes he is very wary indeed. After all, he knows the tangles that happen in fairy stories!

THE AIR-RAID SHELTER
Jeremy Strong

Adam and his sister Rachel find a perfect place for their secret camp in the grounds of a deserted house, until they are discovered by their sworn enemies and things go from bad to worse.